CALGARY PUBLIC LIBRARY

Skunks

Skunks

Sandra Lee
THE CHILD'S WORLD®, INC.

Copyright © 1999 by The Child's World®, Inc.
All rights reserved. No part of this book may be
reproduced or utilized in any form or by any means
without written permission from the publisher.
Printed in the United States of America.

Library of Congress Cataloging-in-Publication Data
Lee, Sandra.
Skunks / by Sandra Lee.
p.   cm.
Includes index.
Summary: A simple introduction to the physical
characteristics, behavior, life cycle, and habitat of skunks.
ISBN 1-56766-503-9 (lib. reinforced : alk paper)
1. Skunks—Juvenile literature.
[1. Skunks.]   I. Title.
QL737.C25L445   1998
599.76'8—dc21   97-43375
CIP
AC

Photo Credits

ANIMALS ANIMALS © Richard Day: 2
ANIMALS ANIMALS © Zig Leszczynski: 13, 23
ANIMALS ANIMALS © E.R.Degginger: 15
ANIMALS ANIMALS © Jack Wilburn: 29
© 1996 Anthony Mercieca/Dembinsky Photo Assoc. Inc: 6, 30
© Daniel J. Cox/Natural Exposures: 9, 10, 19, 24
© Dwight Kuhn: 16
© 1996 Jim Battles/Dembinsky Photo Assoc. Inc: 20
© Renee Lynn/Tony Stone Images: cover
© 1992 Skip Moody/Dembinsky Photo Assoc. Inc: 26

On the cover...

Front cover: This *striped skunk* is walking in the snow.
Page 2: This young striped skunk is exploring a field of flowers.

Table of Contents

Chapter	Page
Meet the Skunk!	7
What Do Skunks Look Like?	8
What Are Skunks?	11
Are There Different Kinds of Skunks?	14
Where Do Skunks Live?	18
What Are Baby Skunks Like?	21
What Do Skunks Eat?	22
Are Skunks Important?	25
Do Skunks Have Any Enemies?	27
Are Skunks Dangerous?	28
Index & Glossary	32

Meet the Skunk!

Imagine that you are walking in a nighttime forest. Fireflies glow in the trees. In the distance, an owl hoots softly. Suddenly, you hear a rustling noise from some nearby bushes. As you watch, a black animal with a white stripe climbs out. It sniffs the air and moves along. What could this creature be? It's a skunk!

⇐ This skunk is out for a nighttime walk.

What Do Skunks Look Like?

When you see a skunk, you might feel like going up and petting it. After all, skunks are beautiful animals. Most of them are about the size of a large cat. They have soft, shiny black fur with pretty markings. Their tails are long and bushy. But petting skunks is not a good idea! In fact, if you see a skunk, you should leave it alone. Skunks can be dangerous if they get frightened.

It is easy to see why many people think skunks are cute animals. ⇒

What Are Skunks?

Skunks belong to a group of animals called **mustelids**. Weasels, minks, badgers, and otters are mustelids, too. All of these animals have a secret weapon they use when they get frightened. Pouches at the base of their tails spray a sticky, smelly liquid called **musk**. A skunk's musk smells terrible! The strong smell can last for days.

⇐ This skunk is taking a walk during the day.

Skunks spray their musk only when they have to. First, the frightened skunk stamps its front feet to warn its enemy away. Then it raises its tail and walks along with very stiff legs. One kind of skunk, the *spotted skunk*, even does a handstand! If these warnings do not work, the skunk arches its back and sprays its musk.

With its tail high and forward, this skunk is ready to spray its musk. ⇒

Are There Different Kinds of Skunks?

There are three different kinds of skunks. *Spotted skunks* have large white spots all over their bodies. They are smaller than other skunks and can climb trees. *Hog-nosed skunks* look very different. They have bare noses and no stripes on their faces. They spend their lives on the ground.

This *spotted skunk* wants to be left alone. ⇒

The most common kind of skunk is the *striped skunk*. Striped skunks live in many areas of the United States. They also live in Mexico and southern Canada. Striped skunks have black bodies with white stripes down their backs. They also have white fur on their heads. They have small ears and little noses. Like other skunks, their legs are short and thick.

⇐ This striped skunk is trying to get a closer look at a plant.

Where Do Skunks Live?

Forests, prairies, and deserts are all places where skunks live. The skunks make cozy homes, or **dens**, under fallen trees or inside hollow logs. Some skunks use dens left behind by other animals. Skunks keep their dens warm and dry by lining them with dry leaves and grasses. There they sleep and raise their babies.

This skunk family has made its den inside a hollow log.

What Are Baby Skunks Like?

In the spring the baby skunks, called **kittens**, are born. Usually, the mother has about six kittens at one time. The babies are black and white and very tiny. For two months, the kittens drink only their mother's milk. Slowly they grow bigger and stronger. When they are old enough, their mother teaches them how to hunt for food. She also teaches them how to stay safe outside of the den.

⇐ This skunk kitten is exploring its surroundings.

What Do Skunks Eat?

Skunks are mostly **nocturnal** animals, which means that they are active at night and sleep during the day. At night, skunks can find many of their favorite foods. Worms, beetles, mice, grasshoppers, and crickets are all things skunks like to eat. They also eat fruits, berries, and grains. If a skunk is really hungry, it might even break into a farmer's henhouse and steal some eggs.

This hungry skunk is eating a deer mouse. ⇒

Are Skunks Important?

Skunks love to eat insects and other animals that can be pests. Be eating the insects that damage farmer's crops, skunks help the crops grow healthy and strong. And by eating mice and worms that attack the harvested grains, skunks help farmers even more. Without skunks, farmers would have lots of problems.

⇐ This skunk is getting ready to hunt for worms.

Do Skunks Have Any Enemies?

Many animals leave skunks alone, but others hunt skunks for food. Hawks and bobcats eat skunks if they are hungry enough. Great-horned owls are the skunk's worst enemy. Their huge size and silent wings help them sneak up on careless skunks and carry them away. In fact, some great-horned owls eat skunks so often, they smell like skunk musk!

⇐ This great-horned owl is resting on a tree branch.

Are Skunks Dangerous?

If you ever see a skunk in the wild, leave it alone! The skunk does not want to be bothered and might think you are trying to hurt it. Just stay quiet and still until it wanders away. Otherwise you might get sprayed with its smelly musk. The skunk might try to scratch or bite you, too.

Some skunks also carry diseases. One disease, called *rabies*, is very dangerous. People who are bitten by skunks with rabies can get very sick. If you ever get bitten, tell an adult right away. Wash the bite and get to a doctor as soon as you can.

This skunk is looking for food during the night. ⇒

Even though skunks can be dangerous at times, they are still very important animals. They eat insects and other pests that would otherwise bother people. So the next time you are walking in a forest at night, be sure to look for skunks. If you watch them from a safe distance, they are some of nature's most interesting animals.

⇐ This striped skunk is busy eating some insects.

Glossary

dens (DENZ)
Dens are animals' homes. Skunks make their dens inside hollow logs or under fallen trees.

kittens (KIT-tenz)
Baby skunks are called kittens. Mother skunks usually have about six kittens at a time.

musk (MUSK)
Musk is a smelly liquid skunks use to protect themselves. They spray the musk at their enemies.

mustelids (MUH-steh-lidz)
Mustelids are animals that produce strong-smelling musk. Skunks, otters, weasels, minks, and badgers are all mustelids.

nocturnal (nok-TUR-null)
Nocturnal animals are active at night and sleep during the day. Skunks are nocturnal.

Index

appearance, 7-8
dangers of, 8, 28
defense, 11-12
dens, 18
different kinds, 14
enemies, 27
food, 22
hog-nosed skunk, 14
importance, 25
kittens, 21
location, 18
musk, 11-12, 27-28
mustelids, 11
nocturnal, 22
rabies, 28
spotted skunk, 12, 14
striped skunk, 17